# The Garden on Gre

by Meish Goldish • illustrated by Judy Jarrett

SCHOLASTIC INC.
New York   Toronto   London   Auckland   Sydney
Mexico City   New Delhi   Hong Kong   Buenos Aires

Developed by Kirchoff/Wohlberg, Inc., in cooperation with Scholastic Inc.

8  9  10                    40                09  08  07  06

Everybody on our block really cares about the neighborhood. That's why we started the garden on Green Street. It grows where an empty lot used to be. It used to look awful here.

Before the garden, people left trash in the lot. You wouldn't believe the junk that piled up there. There were old car tires and broken bottles. There were old tables and chairs. Anything that people didn't want ended up on our block.

Finally, neighbors decided to do something. They decided to fix up the lot.

First, we carried out all the trash. Then we put in fresh dirt and began to plant.

Some of us planted flowers. My family bought flower seeds from a store. Other families ordered seeds from catalogues. We planted our seeds in one part of the lot.

Other neighbors planted vegetables. Some planted rows of peas, beans, and carrots. Others planted rows of corn, lettuce, and tomatoes. They put up scarecrows to keep birds out of the garden.

By the summertime, the flowers and plants had bloomed. It made the whole block beautiful.

People came from all over town to see the garden. Even the mayor came. A man from the newspaper took pictures. We were famous!

In July, we held a block party. Everyone from the neighborhood showed up. We ate vegetables from the garden. Children painted pictures of the flowers with finger paints. People sang and danced and laughed.

Then the bad news came. One day, we read a story in the newspaper. It said that a company had bought the lot. The company planned to build a parking lot there.

Everyone on our block was very upset. Could they do that to our garden? Could they dig it up and put up a parking lot? It just didn't seem fair.

We needed to do something fast. People on Green Street called a meeting for the next night. They told everyone on the block to come. More than fifty neighbors showed up.

At the meeting, people spoke up loudly.

"It's not right to take away our garden!" one woman shouted.

"We worked hard to build that garden!" a man yelled. Other people in the room clapped and whistled.

Then the meeting leader spoke. "We are going to fight this every way we can," she said. "We will talk to a lawyer to see what to do. There are things that all of us can do right now, too."

"What's that?" someone asked.

The meeting leader explained. "This Saturday, we will hold a march in front of the garden. We must let everyone know that we don't want the parking lot."

"Should we bring anything to the march?" a man asked.

"Yes," the leader said. "Bring signs to carry. Write messages on them. We must show people that we don't want a parking lot. Also, write letters to our town mayor. Tell him why we wish to keep our garden. Make him see how important it is."

The next night, I sat in my room at home. I thought about messages to write. I wrote:

"We Need Our Garden Lot a Lot!"

"Don't Let Cars Drive Away Our Garden!"

"No Parking in the Garden!"

"Let's Keep Green Street Clean!"

Everyone in my family helped out. We took large pieces of cardboard and dark crayons. We made one sign for each of us. We glued a long stick to each sign. That way, the sign could be held high at the march.

Next, I wrote a letter to our town mayor:

Dear Mr. Mayor:

I live on Green Street. We have a beautiful garden here. I know you have seen it. You visited here after it opened.

Now a company wants to tear down our garden. They want to build a parking lot instead. Our garden is prettier than a parking lot. Please don't let them take our garden away.

Sincerely,

Ann Jones

On Saturday, we held our march. It seemed like everyone in the neighborhood showed up. Most people carried signs. My family carried the signs we had made.

At the march, our lawyer spoke to the crowd. She said that a judge would hear our case soon. We were going to court!

People from the TV station and newspaper also showed up. They talked to neighbors who were marching. They asked what the march was all about. Later, I listened to one of the television newscasters report about our garden.

"This is Ted Redhook. This afternoon, more than fifty people marched on Green Street. They're very angry about a company's plan to dig up their neighborhood garden. The company wants to build a parking lot.

"I spoke with many people here today. One man told me, 'This garden is special. It shows how beautiful a neighborhood can be.

"However, the Buildwell Company says that they own the lot and can do what they like with it. Now a judge must decide. This is Ted Redhook, for KABA News."

For a week, nothing happened. Then, the next Saturday, we got a big surprise. Workers from the company showed up at our garden lot. They brought two bulldozers with them. Word spread quickly in the neighborhood.

"Workers are at the garden! They're about to tear everything down! Come quickly!"

In just a few minutes, thirty neighbors had raced to the garden. Workers sat in their bulldozers, ready to drive across the garden.

One man yelled, "Block the bulldozers! Block the bulldozers! Stand in front of them! They can't move if we're in front of them."

All thirty of us lined up. We stretched from one end of the garden to the other. We stood side by side, holding hands. It looked like the way we play "Red Rover" in the schoolyard. Only now, it wasn't a game.

The workers sat in the bulldozers. I knew the scarecrows wouldn't scare them away. I wasn't sure what would happen next.

Soon, many police cars filled the street.

"What's going on here?" an officer asked.

"Those workers are determined to dig up our garden," a man explained.

The officer walked over to one of the workers. "Do you have the right to dig here?" she asked.

The worker pulled a piece of paper from his pocket. He showed it to the officer. The officer walked back to us.

"Sorry, folks," she said, "but these men have the right to dig. The court says so."

Everyone let out a groan.

"Please, don't let them!" a woman begged.
"Our garden is so beautiful!"

The officer shook her head. "I'm sorry, but the
law is the law."

The workers started the bulldozers. Just then,
a car raced down Green Street. It stopped at the
garden. A lawyer jumped out of the car. She waved
a paper at the officer.

"Stop!" she cried. "Here is the judge's new
order. The owner of another lot will sell it for the
parking lot. This garden is saved!"

A big cheer went up from the crowd. We all stood and watched the bulldozers drive away. After that, the police left too. So did the lawyer. Soon, just our neighbors were left.

I looked at the garden for a long time. I was very glad it was still around. It looked even more beautiful to me than ever.

A thought struck me: A neighborhood is like a garden. If everyone works hard at it, beautiful things can happen there. That's the lesson I learned from our garden on Green Street.